The Traveling Taco: The Amazing & Surprising Journey of Many of Your Favorite Foods
Text copyright © 2025 Mia Wenjen
Illustrations copyright © 2025 Kimberlie Clinthorne-Wong
Published in 2025 by Red Comet Press, LLC, Brooklyn, NY

All rights reserved. No part of this book may be used or reproduced in any manner whatsoever without written permission except in the case of brief quotations embodied in critical articles and reviews.

Library of Congress Control Number: 2024939786

ISBN (HB): 978-1-63655-131-9
ISBN (EBOOK): 978-1-63655-132-6

25 26 27 28 29 TLF 10 9 8 7 6 5 4 3 2 1

First Edition
Manufactured in Hong Kong using FSC paper
Red Comet Press is distributed by ABRAMS, New York

RedCometPress.com

THE TRAVELING TACO

THE AMAZING & SURPRISING JOURNEY OF MANY OF YOUR FAVORITE FOODS

MIA WENJEN   KIMBERLIE CLINTHORNE-WONG

RED COMET PRESS • BROOKLYN

Recipes are created to delight and to nourish.
When a recipe travels, new minds help it flourish.

Popular foods can evolve over time.
Cooks add small changes that make them sublime.

AL PASTOR TACO

WHAT IS IT?

There are many different types of tacos in Mexico. The al pastor taco is a particularly complicated one. Meat, usually pork, is marinated, then stacked into a cone shape on a vertical spit and grilled. Slices of the meat are carved, wrapped in corn tortillas, and served with sliced onion, grilled pineapple, cilantro, and sauces.

DID YOU KNOW?

The cone of stacked meat, called the "trompo," can weigh more than 60 pounds before it is cooked!

Heaped in a tortilla, meat flavored with spice, an al pastor taco is sure to entice!

WHERE DOES IT COME FROM?

In the 1930s, immigrants from Lebanon moved to Puebla, Mexico, where they introduced shawarma, a cone of grilled, marinated meat, usually made with lamb.

HOW DID IT CHANGE?

In Mexico, the meat used was eventually switched from lamb to pork. The spices are also different in shawarma versus the al pastor taco. Shawarma seasonings include cumin, turmeric, and paprika. The al pastor taco is usually marinated in chili peppers, spices, and pineapple.

PASTA

Chinese chefs hand-pull pasta into long, skinny strings. Italians shape pasta into all kinds of things!

WHAT IS IT?
Mac 'n' cheese. Spaghetti and meatballs. Pasta needs no introduction! Pasta is usually made with just flour, water, and eggs.

WHERE DOES IT COME FROM?
Noodles existed in China more than 3,200 years ago. Although it's a popular belief that Marco Polo introduced pasta to Italian CE, there is evid introd

HOW DID IT CHANGE?

Italians make their pasta from 100 percent durum wheat, also called semolina flour, which is higher in protein than the flour typically used around the world for pastas.

DID YOU KNOW?

Italians have created over 1,300 shapes of pasta!

CEVICHE

Ceviche is typically made of raw fish cured in lime juice for a light, tasty dish.

WHAT IS IT?
Ceviche is a seafood dish made from raw seafood marinated in lemon or lime juice and seasoned with onions, chili pepper, and spices.

WHERE DOES IT COME FROM?
It's hotly debated where ceviche originates, but it is broadly believed to be from Peru, though in a different form.

PERU

HOW DID IT CHANGE?
Nearly 2,000 years ago, the Incas soaked raw fish for hours in a fermented corn beverage called chicha. The Moche civilization, who lived in northern Peru from 100 to 800 CE, used the juice of a local passionfruit called tumbo to "cook" raw fish. When the Spanish arrived around 400 years ago, they brought citrus and cilantro with them, and the tumbo

DID YOU KNOW?
In Peru, June 28 is National Ceviche Day.

was replaced with sour orange or lime. Japanese people immigrated to Peru around 1899 to work in the sugar cane fields, and they shortened the marinating time and added soy sauce and ginger as flavor ingredients.

CHEESECAKE

Ancient Olympians first tried cheesecake as an energy snack when taking a break.

WHAT IS IT?
Cheesecake is a sweet cheese-based dessert nestled in a cookie crust, and it comes in countless varieties!

HOW DID IT CHANGE?

The ancient Greeks crushed cheese and mixed it with flour, egg, and honey, then baked it in an oven. This ancient Greek dessert was considered a delicacy and served at weddings or as an offering to the gods.

WHERE DOES IT COME FROM?

While New York cheesecake is a famous version that is dense and creamy, cheesecake did *not* originate in New York! In fact, cheesecake can be traced back to Greece and the first Olympic games!

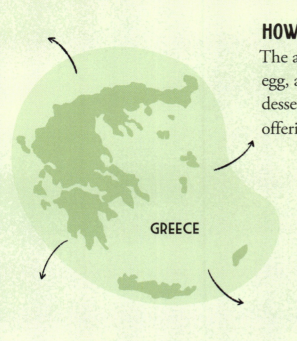

GREECE

DID YOU KNOW?

In the 1870s, a New York dairy farmer tried to recreate soft French cheese and ended up inventing cream cheese instead. Restaurant owner Arnold Ruben, in the 1920s, is credited with inventing New York-style cheesecake, which has cream cheese as the main ingredient!

PAVLOVA

A fruit-topped meringue cake, lighter than air, named after a dancer who jetéd* with flair.

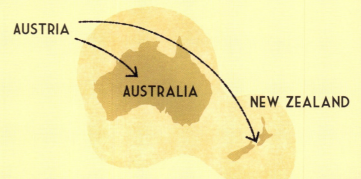

AUSTRIA → AUSTRALIA → NEW ZEALAND

WHAT IS IT?

Typically topped with fresh fruit, pavlova is a meringue cake made from whipped egg whites, cream, and sugar. The crisp outer crust contrasts with the soft, puffy interior.

WHERE DOES IT COME FROM?

Both Australia and New Zealand claim that pavlova was invented in their country and named after Anna Pavlova, a Russian ballet dancer who toured Australia and New Zealand in the 1920s. Food scholars, however, trace the origins of this dessert to an Austrian soufflé cake dating back to the 1770s.

HOW DID IT CHANGE?

Prior to the pavlova cakes created by chefs in Australia and New Zealand, the meringue cakes were hard and crusty. The latest version has the addition of cornstarch to make the pavlova's interior pillowy soft without collapsing.

DID YOU KNOW?

During the Napoleonic Wars in the early 1800s, people migrated to escape war and brought their pavlova-like desserts with them. Before World War II, the German immigrants who moved to Australia brought schaum torte, a similar dessert to pavlova that does not contain cornstarch.

*Jeté: a ballet jump where the dancer leaps into a full split in the air.

FRENCH FRIES

Between France and Belgium, French fries cause tension. Both think that fries are their country's invention.

WHAT IS IT?

French fries are sliced and deep-fried potatoes. In Britain, they are called chips. But the rest of the world knows them as French fries.

WHERE DOES IT COME FROM?

Belgians claim that when the River Meuse froze in 1680, the people who deep-fried little fish along the bank substituted sliced potatoes, thereby creating the "French fry." American soldiers stationed in French-speaking Wallonia during World War I named the fried potato a "French fry," and the name stuck.

UNITED STATES ← BELGIUM

HOW DID IT CHANGE?

Potatoes were introduced to France by the Spanish at the beginning of the sixteenth century, but the French people regarded potatoes with suspicion until 1785, when potatoes were widely eaten due to famine. Thomas Jefferson, who lived in France from 1784 to 1798, is credited with bringing the French fry to America.

DID YOU KNOW?

Belgium is currently petitioning the United Nations Educational, Scientific and Cultural Organization (UNESCO) to recognize the fry as a cultural treasure of Belgium, but France also claims the fried potato as its own.

FISH AND CHIPS

To escape the Inquisition, Jews left by ship, landing in Britain to invent fish and chips.

WHAT IS IT?
Deep-fried, battered fish and French fries, which the British call chips, is a food pairing that is often associated with Britain, but it actually has Jewish roots!

WHERE DOES IT COME FROM?
In 1863, Joseph Malin, a Jewish immigrant fleeing the Portuguese Inquisition, started the first fish-and-chip shop in London.

HOW DID IT CHANGE?
To keep Kosher, Jewish cooks used oil or chicken fat for deep-frying latkes and doughnuts. When they arrived in London, they fried fish and chips in oil, even though it was more expensive than lard. Their version was more delicious and became ubiquitous.

DID YOU KNOW?
Thomas Jefferson tried fish and chips in London, describing it as "fish in the Jewish fashion."

ICE CREAM

Ice cream has roots as a cold royal treat, creamy desserts to enjoy in the heat.

WHAT IS IT?
We all scream for ice cream! Ice cream is a frozen dessert made with cream or milk, sugar, and flavorings.

CHINA

WHERE DOES IT COME FROM?
All over the world and throughout history, people have enjoyed frozen treats, but it's not clear who invented ice cream, or when. The first ice cream, called koumiss, was made from cow, goat, or buffalo milk heated with flour, and was eaten by emperors of the Tang dynasty (618 to 907 CE).

DID YOU KNOW?
Augustus Jackson, a free Black man and presidential chef for James Monroe, John Quincy Adams, and Andrew Jackson, invented the modern method of making ice cream in 1830, using salt mixed with ice to lower and control the temperature.

HOW DID IT CHANGE?

In the eleventh century, the Persians created sharbat, the closest ancestor to ice cream. Icy treats spread to Europe through the Crusades, eventually reaching America.

JERK CHICKEN

High in the mountains, jerk was created,
a way to resist after being invaded.

WHAT IS IT?
Jerk is a method of preparing meat, such as chicken and pork, in a spice marinade followed by smoking and grilling.

WHERE DOES IT COME FROM?
The Caribbean Taíno are credited with creating jerk seasoning using indigenous ingredients including allspice, salt, and spicy bird peppers, which are in the same family as cayenne peppers.

JAMAICA

HOW DID IT CHANGE?
An escaped tribe of enslaved Africans, later known as the Maroons, added to the recipe by smoking whole wild pigs in the Taíno jerk marinade. The Maroons could not risk detection from cooking fires so they used an underground smokeless pit method to make the meat into portable and long-lasting jerky.

DID YOU KNOW?
The Indigenous Taíno migrated from South America to Jamaica by the end of the fifteenth century. In 1494, when the Spanish colonized Jamaica, the Taíno population decreased dramatically from disease and enslavement.

RICE PUDDING

A comforting dish of sweet creamy rice, sprinkled with nuts and cinnamon spice.

WHAT IS IT?
Rice pudding is a delicious dish made of milk, rice, sugar, and often flavored with fruit and spices such as raisins and cinnamon. It can be eaten as a meal or dessert.

HOW DID IT CHANGE?
Rice pudding possibly spread from India to other parts of the world, including Europe, the Middle East, Africa, and the Americas. Every culture seems to have their own version of rice pudding.

WHERE DOES IT COME FROM?
It's a mystery where rice pudding originated from, but India's rice pudding, known as kheer, dates back to 6000 BCE.

INDIA

DID YOU KNOW?
Sombi is a rice pudding that originated in Senegal.

PIZZA

Pizza is ordered by the pie or the slice, an open-faced sandwich at a very good price.

WHAT IS IT?
Pizza is a flattened dough spread with a savory mixture, usually including tomatoes and cheese, and then baked.

WHERE DOES IT COME FROM?
Leavened flatbread topped with something savory such as cheese, herbs, or onions dates back more than 2,000 years to ancient Greece, Egypt, and Rome.

GREECE

EGYPT

ITALY

HOW DID IT CHANGE?

In 1552, the introduction of tomatoes from the Americas to Europe birthed the modern-day pizza in Naples, Italy.

DID YOU KNOW?

Pizza is one of the most popular foods in the world. Every year, people eat more than 5 billion pizzas.

CHURROS

Sometimes dipped in chocolate, this tube-shaped fried dough is known the world over as the delicious churro!

WHAT IS IT?
A churro is piped sweet dough that is fried in hot oil and then sprinkled with sugar.

WHERE DOES IT COME FROM?
There are different theories of where the churro originated, but the oldest references date back to the eighth and ninth century in the Middle East where there are piped doughnut recipes similar to the churro.

DID YOU KNOW?
The Chinese youtiao doughnut is similar to a churro, but it's not piped, covered in sugar, or dunked in chocolate.

HOW DID IT CHANGE?
The earliest recipes are similar to today's churro made from flour, water, and salt but were typically dunked in syrup instead of sprinkled with spiced sugar.

FISH AND CHIPS

FRENCH FRIES

AL PASTOR TACO

CHURROS

JERK CHICKEN

CEVICHE

The Amazing & Surprising Journey of Your Favorite Foods

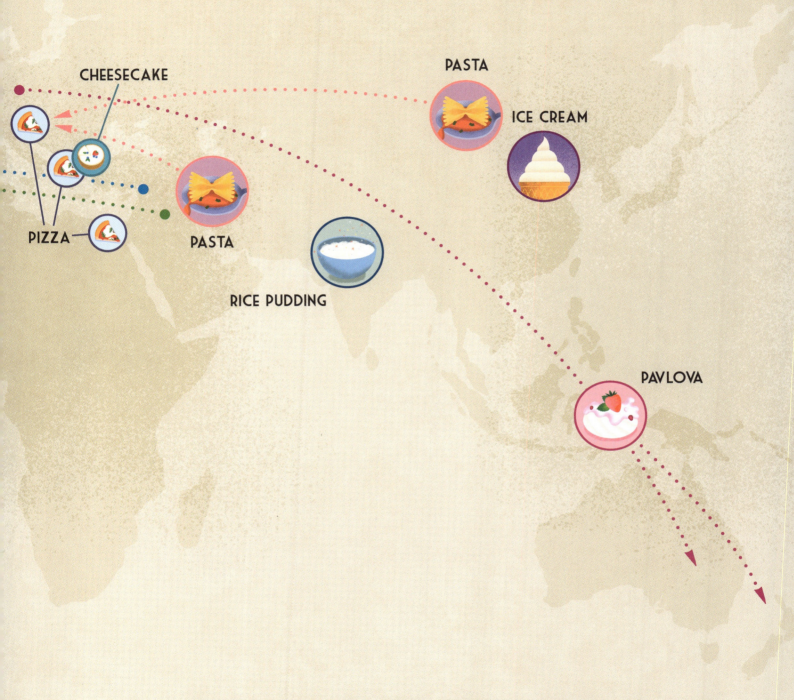

HOW MANY OF THESE FOODS HAVE YOU TRIED?
WHAT ARE YOUR FAVORITE FOODS?
WHERE ARE PLACES YOU HAVE TRAVELED TO?

MIA WENJEN (Author) blogs about parenting, children's books, and education at pragmaticmom.com. She is the cocreator of Multicultural Children's Book Day/Read Your World. She is the author of several illustrated children's books, including *We Sing from the Heart*, also from Red Comet Press. Mia lives in Boston with her husband and three kids. Follow her at @PragmaticMom on X, Instagram, Pinterest, and Facebook.

KIMBERLIE CLINTHORNE-WONG (Illustrator) in addition to being an illustrator, is a designer and ceramicist from Hawaii. She received a BFA in drawing from the University of Hawaii at Manoa and a BFA in illustration from Art Center College of Design in Pasadena, California. She has illustrated several picture books and currently lives and works in Ann Arbor, Michigan.

BIBLIOGRAPHY

Avey, Tori. "Explore the Delicious History of Ice Cream." PBS.org. July 10, 2012. Accessed March 7, 2023.

Benjamin, Sharon. "Rice pudding and its 8000-year-old journey." GulfNews.com. December 26, 2021. Accessed March 7, 2023.

Brown, Miranda. "Did Churros Come from China? A Historian's Refutation of the News (ASIAN 258)." Chinesefoodhistory.org. February 17, 2021. Updated February 24, 2022. Accessed March 7, 2023.

"Ceviche: The National Dish of Peru." PeruforLess.com. March 23, 2021. Accessed March 4, 2023.

Fein, Ronnie. "The surprising Jewish history behind fish n' chips." TimesofIsrael.com. November 13, 2019. Accessed March 6, 2023.

Gray, Vaughn Stafford. "A Brief History of Jamaican Jerk." SmithsonianMagazine.com. December 22, 2020. Accessed March 7, 2023.

"The International Origins of Pasta." Toscanasi.com. Accessed March 2, 2023.

Monaco, Emily. "Can Belgium Claim Ownership of the French Fry?" BBC.com. July 31, 2018. Accessed March 6, 2023.

"Origin of a Classic: Cheesecake." BakeFromScratch.com. Accessed March 4, 2023.

"The Truth Behind Tacos Al Pastor." TastingTable.com. Accessed March 3, 2023.

"The surprising truth about pavlova's origins." BBC.com. August 5, 2020. Accessed March 5, 2023.

"Who Invented Pizza? Did you know pizza took the United States by storm before it became popular in its native Italy?" History.com. July 27, 2012. Updated January 5, 2021. Accessed March 7, 2023.